For the libraries where I did my homework,
laughed with friends and found magic – J.C.

For Sonny and Teddy – F.L.

First published in Great Britain in 2017 by
Andersen Press Ltd., 20 Vauxhall Bridge Road, London SW1V 2SA.
Text copyright © Joseph Coelho 2017. Illustration copyright © Fiona Lumbers 2017.
The rights of Joseph Coelho and Fiona Lumbers to be identified as the author and illustrator of
this work have been asserted by them in accordance with the Copyright, Designs and Patents Act, 1988.
All rights reserved. Printed and bound in China. First edition.
British Library Cataloguing in Publication Data available. ISBN 978-1-78344-548-6

Luna
Loves
Library Day

Joseph Coelho

Fiona Lumbers

Andersen Press

Luna loves library day.

Library bag – check.
Library card – check.
Books to return – check.

Mum drops Luna off at the library.

Dad is always waiting with his head in a book.

Today they start in the
big book section.

THE BIG BOOK OF
DINOSAURS, MUMMIES AND
UNEXPLAINED MYSTERIES.
In the book bag it goes – check.

Luna loves bugs. Dad hates bugs.
They make his face go all
errrnnnngggggggg!
There are bug books with ants, spiders and...

Maurice Mandible's Mini Monsters.
In the book bag it goes — check.

Dad knows lots of magic tricks,
like how to make coins appear from
Luna's nose and ears.

Dad knows how to disappear.
Luna wants to learn
how to bring him back.

Marabella's Book of
MAGIC MAYHEM
In the book bag it goes — check.

Dad finds a history book about where he grew up,
where he used to play and the library he used to go to.

All the photos are black and white.
All the trees look strange.

In the book bag
it goes – check.

Luna chooses a fairy tale to read with Dad
on the big library chair, as soft as a teddy's hug.

THE
TROLL KING
AND THE
MERMAID QUEEN

"I'm the King, the Troll King,
married to the Mermaid Queen."

"I'm the Queen,
the Mermaid Queen,
married to the Troll King."

"I'm the Princess,
the wave-surfing Princess.
My mother is a mermaid,
my father is a troll.
I can swim in any ocean,
I'm at home in any hole."

The mermaid and troll would argue,
though their love for their princess was deep.
Mermaids like splishing and splashing -
trolls like thundering their feet.

Their home became a swell of sounds -
crashing waves, banging boulders,
a chaotic clatter of growls and gurgles
of goats and fish and so...

... the Troll King left.
But one thing always
remained the same:

"My love for my princess daughter
swells my heart with the force of the tides.
My love for my princess daughter
has depths that no hole can hide."

~ THE END ~

Luna checks out her books:

UNEXPLAINED MYSTERIES – check.

Mini Monsters – check.

MAGIC MAYHEM – check.

MEMORIES OF THE
IMAGINED ISLAND – check.

THE TROLL KING AND THE
MERMAID QUEEN – check.

A book bag full of memories
about adventure, magic...
and Dad. Check.

Luna loves library day.

luna's library

Marabella's Book of MAGIC MAYHEM

M. Mandible's MINI MONSTERS

MEMORIES of the Imagined Island

The BIG BOOK of DINOSAURS, MUMMIES
and UNEXPLAINED MYSTERIES